TANA HOBAN

Cubes, Cones, Cylinders, & Spheres

GREENWILLOW BOOKS
An Imprint of HarperCollinsPublishers

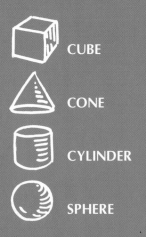

CUBE

CONE

CYLINDER

SPHERE

For Shellie

The full-color photographs were reproduced from 35-mm slides.

Cubes, Cones, Cylinders, & Spheres
Copyright © 2000 by Tana Hoban
All rights reserved. Printed in Singapore by Tien Wah Press.
www.harperchildrens.com

Library of Congress Cataloging-in-Publication Data
Hoban, Tana.   Cubes, cones, cylinders, & spheres / by Tana Hoban.
    p.   cm.   "Greenwillow Books."
Summary: Photographs of all kinds of familiar objects
depict a variety of shapes, including cubes, cones, and spheres.
ISBN 0-688-15325-9 (trade).   ISBN 0-688-15326-7 (lib. bdg.)
1. Geometry—Pictorial works—Juvenile literature. [1. Shape.] I. Title.
QA445.5.H623 2000   516'.15-dc21   99-052909

1 2 3 4 5 6 7 8 9 10   First Edition

BOOKS BY TANA HOBAN

A, B, See!

All About Where

Animal, Vegetable, or Mineral?

Big Ones, Little Ones

A Children's Zoo

Colors Everywhere

Construction Zone

Dig, Drill, Dump, Fill

Dots, Spots, Speckles, and Stripes

Exactly the Opposite

I Read Signs

I Read Symbols

I Walk and Read

Is It Larger? Is It Smaller?

Is It Red? Is It Yellow? Is It Blue?

Is It Rough? Is It Smooth? Is It Shiny?

Just Look

Let's Count

Little Elephant *By Miela Ford*

Look Book

Look! Look! Look!

Look Up, Look Down

The Moon Was the Best *By Charlotte Zolotow*

More, Fewer, Less

Of Colors and Things

One Little Kitten

Round & Round & Round

Shadows and Reflections

Shapes, Shapes, Shapes

Spirals, Curves,
        Fanshapes & Lines

Take Another Look

26 Letters and 99 Cents

Board Books

1, 2, 3

Panda, Panda

Red, Blue, Yellow Shoe

What Is It?

White on Black

Blanco en Negro

Black on White

Negro en Blanco

What Is That?